CUENTO
DE LUZ

To our beloved Luna, from Mom and Dad.

— Ariel Andrés Almada & Sonja Wimmer —

This book is printed on **Stone Paper** with silver **Cradle to Cradle™** certification.

Cradle to Cradle™ is one of the most demanding ecological certification systems, awarded to products that have been conceived and designed in an ecologically intelligent way.

Cradle to Cradle™ recognizes that environmentally safe materials are used in the manufacturing of Stone Paper which have been designed for re-use after recycling. The use of less energy in a more efficient way, together with the fact that no water, trees nor bleach are required, were decisive factors in awarding this valuable certification.

Little One
Text © 2019 Ariel Andrés Almada
Illustrations © 2019 Sonja Wimmer
This edition © 2019 Cuento de Luz SL
Calle Claveles, 10 | Urb. Monteclaro | Pozuelo de Alarcón | 28223 | Madrid | Spain
www.cuentodeluz.com
Original title in Spanish: *Hija*
English translation by Jon Brokenbrow
Printed in PRC by Shanghai Chenxi Printing Co., Ltd. August 2019, print number 1695-14
ISBN: 978-84-16733-72-9

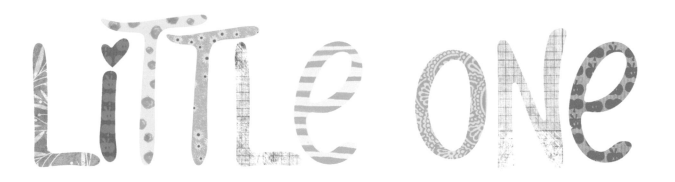

LITTLe ONe

ARIEL ANDRÉS ALMADA & SONJA WIMMER

Wake up, little one.
Open your eyes.

Can you see? Everything around you has been created for you. The clouds that look like snow, and the little sparrow that peeks at you through the window . . .

The smell of pepper that wafts in from the kitchen and tickles your nose; the sound of the wind as it blows through the branches of the almond tree . . . everything has been created so that you can discover it.

But go slowly . . .
It's important to take your time.
If you rush, you'll miss so many things!
Start out by discovering colors, shapes, and sounds.

If you look closely, you'll discover amazing worlds in
even the tiniest things.

And speaking of tiny things, I can see that your mouth is trying to make sounds.

In time, you'll learn that if you put the letters together, you can make words. And if you put the words together, one day you'll wake up and discover that you can talk.

There are so many people in the world who talk differently!

But they all smile the same. Make sure you remember that always, little one.

And another thing . . . I made a note on this wrinkled piece of paper that I had to talk to you about nutshells. Look at the one I've got in my hand, for example.

What do you see when you look at it? Maybe you imagine it's a boat, in which you can explore rivers of the deepest blue.

Or maybe it's a helmet you'll wear when you want to fight for your dreams. Just like nutshells, there are many different ways of seeing the same thing.

And they're all just as important as each other.

As you grow up, you'll discover a whole lot of funny feelings, which we adults call 'emotions.'

Some of them are red, like a ripe apple.

Others are white and fluffy like clouds,
and some shine like stars and fill us with joy.

There are others that are like a stormy sea, and which bring tears to your eyes.

But don't worry, little one. These emotions always disappear
in the end, and your tears will dry when the sun comes out.

I can see on the piece of paper that I have to talk to you about unicorns, too. I saw one once, you know, although I can hardly remember it, because I was very little as well.

As the years went by, I stopped finding them. Sometimes, when we turn into grown-ups, we forget where to look.

But if you see them, don't worry about what other people say. Talk to them, and go off for a ride.

And tell them that I've always wanted to meet them again, and that if they like, they can drop by one night while I'm asleep, and tickle my feet.

So I guess you've got lots of questions you want to ask. So do we!

The thing is, we've got a lot more questions than answers, and so we'll just have to head out and discover things together.

I'll look for the magnifying glass I used when I was little, and we'll start exploring.

Why are you smiling at me like that? Oh yes!
Your parents were little once, too, even if it
seems like it was a long, long time ago

So here's the deal: we'll help you to grow,

and through the eyes of a
child, you'll help us to discover
the world once again.

Okay? Great! Then hold our hands, little one, and as the wind blows through your curls, show us the point on the horizon where you want to take your first steps . . .